water bug

Some **water bug**
can race across the
surface of the water
without getting wet.

spider

Most **spiders**
have eight eyes.

flies

caterpillar

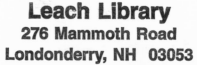

bee

To my three baby sisters,
Helen, Ronny, and Libby,
who never, ever, bugged me!
—P.S.

For my little bug,
Margaret Kate
—S.H.

I Love Bugs!
Text copyright © 2005 by Philemon Sturges
Illustrations copyright © 2005 by Shari Halpern
Manufactured in China.
All rights reserved.
www.harperchildrens.com

Library of Congress Cataloging-in-Publication Data
Sturges, Philemon.
I love bugs! / by Philemon Sturges ;
illustrated by Shari Halpern.—1st ed.   p.   cm.
Summary: A boy extols the various characteristics
of bugs, all of whom he loves.
ISBN 0-06-056168-8 — ISBN 0-06-056169-6 (lib. bdg.)
[1. Insects—Fiction.   2. Stories in rhyme.]
I. Halpern, Shari, ill.   II. Title.
PZ8.3.S9227Iae   2005   [E]—dc22   2004004120

1 2 3 4 5 6 7 8 9 10
❖
First Edition

I Love Bugs!

BY **Philemon Sturges**

ILLUSTRATED BY **Shari Halpern**

HarperCollins *Publishers*

Bugs, bugs, bugs! I like bugs.

Bugs that creep,

bugs that crawl,

bugs that hop

or fly.

I love to find them under rocks

or watch them in the sky.

These bugs paddle.

This one weaves.

Some make honey.

Some chew leaves.

Some bugs burrow underground.

Others swoop and buzz around.

This one's like a bit of bark.

This one's like a twig.

Cicadas buzz a summer song.

Crickets dance a jig.

I like bugs that blink at night

or flutter round the back porch light.

But this bug is the best of all.

It's Ladybug!

She loves to crawl.

Bugs, bugs, bugs! I LOVE bugs!

ant

Some **ants** can carry more than twenty times their own weight!

praying mantis

The **praying mantis** is the only insect that can turn its head halfway around to look over its shoulder.

cicada

Some **cicadas** spend seventeen years underground.

deerfly

The buzzing of a **fly** is the sound of its wings beating.

moth

Unlike butterflies, most **moths** are active at night.